Storybook
Collection

This edition published by Parragon Books Ltd in 2014

Parragon Books Ltd
Chartist House
15–17 Trim Street
Bath BA1 1HA, UK
www.parragon.com

ISBN 978-1-4723-5280-4

Printed in China

Storybook
Collection

Bath • New York • Cologne • Melbourne • Delhi
Hong Kong • Shenzhen • Singapore • Amsterdam

Contents

Meet the Pets

Beauty

Beauty is Aurora's pretty kitty. One of Beauty's favourite things is the little mask she uses to cover her eyes when sleeping during the day. Beauty loves rose perfume, playing in the garden, sleeping on Aurora's lap and dreaming about sunny days.

Berry

Berry is the fluffiest bunny you will ever meet. Much like her princess, Snow White, Berry is gentle, graceful and loves freshly picked blueberries. Berry is a very shy bunny, but if you give her sweets, you'll soon be best friends.

Blondie

Blondie is Rapunzel's brave and loyal pony. She has a very regal look – especially with her beautiful long blonde mane – and she gives the best salutes in all the land! Blondie enjoys spending time with Maximus, her friend and hero, and she loves it when Rapunzel plaits her mane.

Pumpkin

Pumpkin is a glamorous puppy. Her tail is always perfectly styled, her ears are expertly fluffed and she never goes anywhere without her sparkling tiara. Pumpkin loves eating sweets, dancing and attending Royal Balls – just like, Cinderella!

Meet the Pets

Teacup

You will never meet a more talented puppy than Teacup. Whether she's curtsying or balancing treats on her head, this elegant little pup loves practising with Belle and performing for a crowd. One of Teacup's most treasured possessions is a little harp that she often plays for Belle.

Treasure

Treasure is an unusual kitten – she loves water! Before she met Ariel, Treasure loved sneaking on to ships and playing on deck. Just like Ariel, this curious little kitten loves to collect trinkets … she even has her own lucky shell.

Bayou

The Mardi Gras parade is Bayou's favourite time of year. Usually, Bayou is very prim and proper – she is a regal pony, after all! But when Bayou hears the cheerful music, she and Tiana quickly put on their colourful costumes and prance around the parade.

Sultan

Sultan would do anything to protect his beloved Princess Jasmine. No royal tiger is more loyal – he may be small, but his bravery is one million times his size. Sultan enjoys playing around in heaps of royal pillows and silks. But his favourite thing is a present Jasmine gave him – a magic-carpet blanket.

Beauty, the Pretty Kitty Who Loves to Sleep

Beauty loves to sleep in the morning sunshine, the afternoon shade and, of course, the evening moonlight.

The other kittens tease that she needs a prince to wake her.

Little do they know, a princess will....

Princess Aurora is no stranger to sleeping.

It is well known throughout the kingdom that she was once called

Sleeping Beauty and that she was woken from a spell with a kiss.

One day, Aurora is frolicking in the palace garden with her fairy friends. The sweet scent of new roses is spellbinding and she has to use all her willpower not to lie down for a nap.

But her fairy friends aren't ready to rest.

"Look!" Merryweather calls, as she hovers above a rosy tail.

"It's a lion! It's a tiger! It's a dragon!"

But Aurora isn't falling for it. In fact,

she is just about to lay her head down when

Merryweather and Fauna fly over.

"Do take a look," Fauna urges Aurora.

Aurora follows them to the rosy tail.

But it doesn't belong to a lion, or a tiger,

or a dragon …

… it belongs to a sleeping Beauty.

Aurora has never seen such a beautiful kitten before. Her rosy fur shimmers in the sunshine, her little pink nose glows and her purr is like music.

Merryweather and Fauna bounce around

Beauty, trying to wake her with a little magic.

Aurora doesn't want to disturb the kitten.

But it is too late.

Beauty has become aware of a breeze tickling her nose and the warm sun disappearing behind a cloud. She opens her eyes – and sees a princess!

Aurora is sure the surprised kitten will arch her back and hiss.

But Beauty just yawns sweetly then leaps into Aurora's arms.

The princess sings to Beauty until she starts purring and drifts off to sleep again.

The fairies giggle. "You're perfect for each other, dear," says Flora.

Now the two beauties curl up together for long,

luxurious naps – always waking just in time for yummy treats!

Berry, the Sweetest Bunny of Them All

Berry is a shy little bunny. There is only one thing she isn't shy about: blueberries. Berry loves blueberries. That's how she got her sweet name.

It is a bright summer day and Berry's favourite time of year. The bushes are bursting with sweet berries. Berry bounds out of bed for breakfast!

That same bright day, Snow White
and her prince are out picking berries
to bake in a pie for the Seven Dwarfs.

Snow White drops each berry into a silver bucket.

It is nearly full when she comes across a bush with the

biggest blueberries of all!

But Berry isn't going to let those big blueberries go.

Just as Snow White is about to pluck a berry, there is a rustle.

The berry is gone! Snow White reaches for a different berry and

hears another rustle. That berry is gone, too!

Then she catches sight of a fluffy tail, as white as snow,

disappearing into the leaves.

Snow White finds her plumpest berry. Placing it in her palm, she kneels down and waits. Slowly a little bunny peeks out from the blueberry bush.

When Berry sees the princess holding that big, beautiful berry,

she no longer feels shy. She hops on to Snow White's lap to eat more.

Soon, Snow White has to say goodbye.

But Berry isn't going to let that bucket of blueberries go.

She hops after the princess all the way back to the castle.

Imagine Snow White's surprise when she finds Berry hiding in
the bucket. Thankfully, there are enough berries for a pie *and* for Berry!

Now Berry bounds out of bed to have breakfast with her princess.

Today, Snow White has a new treat for her bunny: sweet mashed carrots.

Mirror, mirror, on the wall, who's the sweetest of them all? Berry!

Blondie, the Little Pony with the Big Dream

Blondie is a little pony with a big dream.
She wants to be a royal horse.

When Blondie braves the royal stables, the bigger horses tease her.

"You can't be a royal horse. You're too little!"

But they agree her blonde mane is beautiful.

One very important day, Blondie gets lucky.

The king and queen are throwing a parade to celebrate Rapunzel's return. In the bustle to get ready, Blondie sneaks into the line-up.

Blondie had heard the legend of the lost princess.

Not long ago, she'd seen the most beautiful girl enter the kingdom.

She didn't know then that this was the princess, Rapunzel.

Rapunzel loves parades. Musicians play cheerful tunes, while floats covered in flowers and flags roll by, and the royal horses march.

Rapunzel loves horses. She has wished for one since she was a little girl trapped in a tower. But Rapunzel doesn't just wish for any horse. She is waiting for the right one.

As Blondie marches, she gets a little too excited. She steps on her long mane and bumps into the horse next to her.

Then she stumbles – right in front of the princess!

The royal horses huff and neigh.

Blondie is so embarrassed, she lowers her heavy head.

Slowly Rapunzel makes her way to the little pony.

Everyone holds their breath to see what the princess will do.

When Blondie sees that
Rapunzel is plaiting her long
blonde mane, she is amazed.

Rapunzel's hair is now short
and brown. Blondie wonders if
Rapunzel misses having her
long hair plaited.

When Rapunzel has finished, Blondie feels so loved.

She shakes her head and salutes the princess.

The crowd applauds loudly. Little Blondie has

made a big impression on everyone.

Blondie is now a royal horse. But she's not just any royal horse – she's Rapunzel's royal horse. And she is the proudest pony in the kingdom!

Pumpkin, a Puppy Fit for a Princess

Pumpkin loves to prance. From the moment this little puppy was born, she has wanted to attend royal balls and dance!

50

So when the prince
arrives to pick a puppy
for Cinderella, Pumpkin
decides to make her move.

Standing up on her
hind legs, she twirls and
dances, hops and prances.

The prince knows Cinderella will love a puppy with such pizzazz. He chooses Pumpkin and puts her in a basket. He wants to surprise the princess at their anniversary ball that night.

Soon, it is time for the ball. When the music begins, Pumpkin

cannot wait. She hops out of the basket to stretch her dancing legs.

Cinderella has plenty
to celebrate tonight.

It has been a year since she
rode in an enchanted carriage …

set her foot into
a glass slipper …

and married her prince.

At the ball, Cinderella twirls and dances, dips and prances,

until she and the prince are alone on the dance floor.

The prince asks Cinderella for a final dance

beneath the stars. As they walk on to the balcony,

he glances at the basket – but it is empty!

But the prince has no reason to worry. On the other side of the balcony Pumpkin is twirling and dancing, hopping and prancing.

It only takes a moment for Cinderella

to notice the pretty little puppy.

When the song ends, Cinderella lifts Pumpkin into her arms and thanks her prince for such a wonderful anniversary surprise.

Cinderella and Pumpkin have been together ever since,

attending royal balls and dancing the nights away.

They really are the most perfect pair.

Teacup, the Performing Pup

Every day in the village square, Teacup the pup performs for the villagers, hoping someone will notice her.

Some days she finds it easy to
shine and is rewarded with treats!

On other days Teacup
finds it hard to shine and
hides away.

One bright morning, Teacup is performing her signature

move when she sees a beautiful girl walk by.

But it isn't just any girl – it is Belle!

Teacup has seen the princess from afar before,

but today Belle has stopped to watch her.

Just then, a beam of sunlight catches one of Belle's golden earrings, blinding the peppy little pup.

The teacup on top of her head wobbles, then it topples to the ground and breaks.

The villagers shake their heads in
sympathy and slowly walk away.

But the princess stays. She kneels
down and picks up the broken pieces.

"Don't worry, sweet little pup, I'll help you," says Belle.

Then she carries Teacup home.

At Belle's palace, Teacup is presented with her teacup –

it is perfectly repaired. And there are treats!

Teacup had dreamed of being noticed.

Now she is Belle's little star, performing just for the princess ...

... unless she's performing in the village square,

where she always wears sunglasses!

Treasure, the Kitten Who Loves the Sea

Treasure loves the beach. Every day she plays in the rolling waves and dreams of adventure.

Most cats are afraid of water. But not Treasure!

Treasure is a sweet, brave, playful and, most of all,

curious little kitten.

One day, Treasure feels curious about the sea, so she stows away on a ship.

She dreams of collecting beautiful treasures and trinkets from faraway lands.

Little does Treasure know that she is on Prince Eric's ship! Imagine the royal crew's surprise when they discover a furry little stowaway.

Treasure is just as

surprised – and worried.

Will she have

to scrub the deck?

Will they make

her walk the plank?

No! Prince Eric wants to adopt Treasure and sail the seas with her. The curious kitten with the shiny red fur reminds him of someone he loves very much. And that special someone will be boarding the royal ship later that day!

While the prince leads Princess Ariel aboard, a sea breeze blows a string of shells. Treasure leaps to paw at it and the sound catches Ariel's attention. She turns to see Treasure.

Ariel picks up the kitten and cuddles her close.

Treasure smells of the sea, which makes Ariel very happy.

Treasure purrs softly in the princess's arms.

When the ship returns to the docks,

Treasure follows Ariel to her palace.

Treasure is now Ariel's little treasure and they
collect trinkets and swim together all day long.

Bayou, the Little Pony Who Loves to Prance

Bayou lives in the tiny country of Maldonia, but she is moving to a big city. Prince Naveen's parents are taking her to live with Princess Tiana.

Bayou boards a ship and they set sail for America.

Although she is sad to be leaving her home,

Bayou is excited to see what a big city is like.

After a long ocean voyage, Bayou finally meets the princess
at the Port of New Orleans. Tiana has a surprise for her new pet.

It's a costume!
Bayou has arrived
just in time for the
Mardi Gras parade –
a New Orleans tradition.

But Bayou isn't used to
colourful costumes. She feels
a long way from home.

Luckily, Tiana has just the
thing to make her feel better:
a slice of apple pie Tiana has
baked herself.

The pie is so good that when Bayou hears the parade music begin, she can't help but prance a little.

The Mardi Gras parade is amazing to see.

There are so many bright colours and dazzling lights

that Bayou doesn't know where to look first.

But even better than watching the parade is being in it!

The princess is so happy that her new pony is having fun.

The next day, Tiana introduces Bayou to her friend Charlotte LaBouff. Bayou will be living in the cosy stables at the LaBouff estate.

After Bayou has had a look around the stables, Tiana takes the little pony to her world-class restaurant – Tiana's Palace.

It is Tiana's home away from home and now it is Bayou's, too!

Bayou now adores New Orleans, parades and dressing up. But she adores Princess Tiana even more!

Sultan, the Bravest Tiger of Them All

Sultan might be a little tiger,
but he always tries to be brave.

He spends most of his time roaming in the
jungle, roaring and protecting his friends.

If he isn't prowling in the jungle, Sultan can be found

at the Agrabah market, protecting fancy silk fabrics.

The merchants who work in the market always reward Sultan with a bowl of milk. But what he really wants is a home of his own.

One afternoon, Sultan snuggles up in some silky fabrics for a catnap and is soon dreaming about protecting his own home.

While Sultan is sleeping, Princess Jasmine is wandering through the market. She is looking at all the bright colours, meeting new people and enjoying the scents of spices and freshly cut flowers.

When Jasmine reaches the silk stand, she touches the smooth, cool fabric and imagines a new dress. But when her hand brushes something fluffy ... a little tiger appears!

Sultan is so startled by the princess that he has forgotten to be brave. But Jasmine doesn't mind. She thinks the little tiger is the cutest thing she's ever seen.

Jasmine forgets all about the silks. What she really wants is Sultan. She asks if she can take him home.

The merchant will miss the little tiger but he knows Sultan will have a good life with the princess.

As they leave the market, Jasmine tells Sultan all about her palace. That's when Sultan realizes he is going to have a home of his own!

Sultan might be a little tiger, but he always

protects his beautiful new home – and his princess!

Beauty and Treasure
Take a Dip

Beauty is so happy to be Aurora's pet.
One day, she wakes up from a nap in the
garden and sees a giant butterfly flying overhead!

When the butterfly lands, Beauty leaps after it. But just as she is about to catch it … it flies away again!

Then Beauty notices that it's not a butterfly at all.

It is Aurora's painting
and it's still wet!

When Aurora finds her painting,
she discovers that Beauty has added a
special touch. Now Beauty needs a bath!

While waiting for Aurora to fill the bath tub, Beauty thinks about hiding. She may be a royal kitty, but she's frightened of water.

Suddenly, a hummingbird appears.

"Hi, I'm Shimmer," says the hummingbird.

"Don't be scared. I know a cat who loves water.

Her name is Treasure."

"Come on," says Shimmer. "Let's fly!"

With a hum and a whir, they are off to meet Treasure.

115

Soon, Beauty finds herself on a magical beach.

She has never seen water so pink.

Then she notices Treasure floating in the water –

Beauty has never met a cat who loves water before!

"Swim with me!" says Treasure. Beauty shakes her head. Suddenly, a pretty butterfly flits past. Beauty leaps after it – and lands in the water!

But once Beauty gets used to it, the water feels delightful.

Treasure is having so much fun splashing in the gentle waves …

and now Beauty is, too! Treasure teaches Beauty how to float and

the little kittens have a wonderful time relaxing together.

Soon, it is time for Beauty to go home.

Although she is sad to leave Treasure,

Beauty is excited to see Aurora again.

Beauty waves goodbye to Treasure ...

… and arrives home just in time for her bath!

Beauty is no longer frightened of water. She loves bathtime!

And with every splash, she thinks about her sweet new friend.

Blondie and Berry's Fruitful Friendship

Rapunzel is so happy to have Blondie as her pony. She visits the royal stables every day to brush Blondie's long tail and mane.

One day, Rapunzel brings
a bucket of bright red apples
to the stable for Blondie and
the royal horses to share.

Blondie loves apples! But by
the time she reaches the bucket,
the apples are gone.

The other horses have eaten
them all.

Blondie is a little sad, so she decides to go for a walk.

The sky is bright blue and the air is crisp and sweet.

Suddenly, Blondie spots a shiny red apple.

Then she finds another ... and another.

When Blondie looks up there are apples everywhere!

Now she has more than she can eat! But what Blondie

really wants is a friend to share her treats with.

That's when Blondie looks up and sees a hummingbird flying overhead.

"I'm Shimmer," says the hummingbird. "And I have just the friend for you! Her name is Berry and she loves fruit."

Blondie is excited – she can't wait to meet Berry!

"Let's fly!" says Shimmer and, with a hum and a whir, they are off.

When they land, Blondie finds herself in a magical forest.

She has never seen so many blueberry bushes!

Blondie is looking around in amazement when she hears

a rustle and spots a fluffy white tail poking out from a bush.

Berry's fluffy white tail gives a little shake, then she rolls a single blueberry out to Blondie. And then another … and another! Blondie tastes the berries. They are so sweet and delicious.

"Follow me!" says Berry. "I'll show you where the biggest blueberries are." Together they collect as many as they can find and share them with Berry's forest friends.

Soon, it is time for Blondie to go home.

"Good bye!" she shouts as she flies off. The little pony is sad to

leave her new friends, but she is excited to see her princess again.

And now Blondie knows how to make friends with the royal horses!

After saying goodbye to Shimmer, Blondie heads straight to the apple orchard. She fills a bucket with apples ...

… and shares them with all the other royal horses.

Now Blondie has a stable full of friends!

Teacup and Petit Have Fun in the Forest

Teacup is going to perform in the village square.

The little puppy is running late so she decides to take

a shortcut through the forest.

Teacup skips along the wooded path. The sun is sparkling in the sky, the birds are singing, and little forest animals are playing in the leaves.

"I'm on my way to perform in the village square!" Teacup tells them.

"Will you perform for us first?" asks a chipmunk.

Teacup knows she should get to the village,

but she can't turn down an opportunity to shine!

She picks up a pine cone and balances it on

her head while she dances.

But, from far off in the distance, Teacup hears the village-clock chime. It's time for her performance! If she doesn't leave now, Teacup will be late!

Teacup says goodbye to her friends and continues on her way.

But the further Teacup runs down the wooded path, the darker the forest becomes. Until Teacup realizes she is lost....

Suddenly, Teacup hears rustling and a loud snort. Is it a lion? Is it a bear? Teacup trembles and dashes out of sight.

But it's Petit, Belle's favourite pony!

"Hello, Teacup!" Petit neighs, startled. "Shouldn't you be in the village square?"

"I'm lost," cries Teacup, "and I'm late for my show."

"Well, you can't perform without these," Petit says,

smiling at the sad little puppy.

"My sunglasses!" shouts Teacup. "Thank you."

"Now, jump up," says Petit. "I'll give you a ride."

Then Teacup has a brilliant idea.

When they reach the village, Teacup and Petit make quite an entrance. The waiting crowd claps with delight.

Teacup and Petit put on the best show the villagers have ever seen! Then, as they take a bow, someone shouts, "Bravo!" It's Belle – Teacup and Petit's biggest fan.

On their way home, Teacup, Petit and Belle make a special stop. Teacup wants to finish performing for the forest animals but, this time, she wants Petit to join her!

Treasure's High-seas Adventure

T reasure is playing with her friends Scuttle, Flounder, Sebastian and Max.

As Treasure runs along the shore, she spots a boat at the water's edge!

Being a curious kitten, Treasure leaps inside.

After all, she does love the sea.

"All aboard!" she announces to her friends.

Max and Sebastian are less sure that this is

a good idea, but they would never let Treasure

go alone so they follow her on to the boat.

Treasure imagines that she is on

a high-seas adventure with her friends.

She keeps a lookout for danger, while

her crew work hard to sail the ship.

Then, out of the blue, a big wave rolls on to the beach, lifting their boat and setting them afloat!

It's not imaginary any more – Teacup and her friends really are at sea!

Treasure is very excited – she's always wanted to go on a real adventure.

But Sebastian is worried. "Where are we going?" asks the crab.

"Are those storm clouds?" Max adds, his voice shaking with nerves.

Sure enough, it starts to rain.

"Batten down the hatches!" shouts Treasure. The little kitten is having a wonderful time. But Sebastian and Max just stare nervously at the sky.

Then, suddenly, the rain is pouring down!

Treasure tries to stay brave. She doesn't want Max

and Sebastian to know that she's scared, too!

But just as suddenly as the storm had blown in, it blows out again. The sky clears, the sea becomes calm, and captain and crew are treated to a beautiful rainbow.

Now the storm has passed, Treasure and her crew start to enjoy their time at sea. Eventually, a gentle wave carries their boat back to land.

As soon as his paws touch dry sand, Max runs to Prince Eric.

Treasure follows close behind and is greeted by Ariel.

The princess is not surprised that her curious kitten had

taken to the sea.

Treasure and Max agree that they've had quite enough

adventure for one day, so everyone heads home.

But Treasure is sure she'll be back at sea soon!

The End